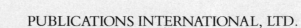

Look and Find
Heroes
and
Legends

Pecos Bill • Tarzan
Johnny Appleseed • King Arthur
Hercules • And more!

Illustrated by Jerry Tiritilli

Illustration script development by David Guy Martino

Louis Weber, C.E.O.
Publications International, Ltd.
7373 North Cicero Avenue
Lincolnwood, Illinois 60646

Manufactured in the U.S.A.

8 7 6 5 4 3 2 1

ISBN 1-56173-419-5

PUBLICATIONS INTERNATIONAL, LTD.

CHECK RICHES HERE

HAVE A NICE DAY!

Robin Hood and his band of Merry Men lived deep in Sherwood Forest. They were wanted by the Sheriff of Nottingham, for they took from the rich and gave to the poor. As more and more people joined Robin Hood, it became difficult to tell the good guys from the bad guys!

First, find Robin Hood and these other good guys:

Robin Hood

Will Scarlet

Little John

Friar Tuck

Maid Marian

Now, find these bad guys:

The Sheriff of Nottingham

Guy of Gisborne

Prince John

VOTE FOR ME

WANTED

WANTED

Somethin' is mighty wrong at the Campground El Largo. Seems Paul Bunyan, the mighty lumberjack, can't find his trusty companion Babe, the Big Blue Ox! And there's a heap o' work to be done.

First, find Paul Bunyan. Then help him find Babe and these other big fellas around the camp.

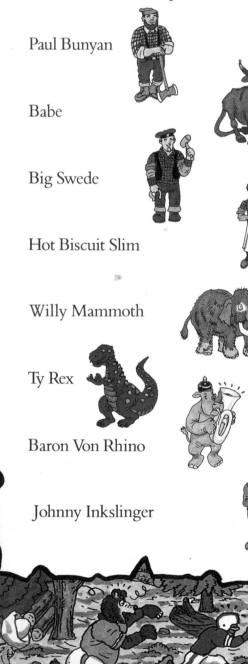

Paul Bunyan

Babe

Big Swede

Hot Biscuit Slim

Willy Mammoth

Ty Rex

Baron Von Rhino

Johnny Inkslinger

A s far back as anyone can reckon, Davy Crockett loved huntin' in the Tennessee hills. With Ol' Betsy by his side, and some o' the strangest pets you ever did see, Davy became the most howliferous feller ever to wear a coonskin cap!

After you find Davy, look for his pets and hunting things.

Davy Crockett

Ol' Betsy

Davy's powder horn

A slingshot

Mississip'

A spear

Sherlock Hound

Mile-A-Minute

Huggie

Orphaned in the jungles of Africa, young Lord Greystoke was adopted and raised by a couple of real swingers! Tarzan (as he is known to those with whom he "hangs out") ruled the jungle with Jane, his wife, and their twins, Boy and Girl.

Can you find Tarzan? Look for these other folks with a jungle address, too!

Tarzan

Jane

Boy and Girl

Anna Conda

King Leo

Aunt Polly

Toucan Lou

Bongo the Chimp

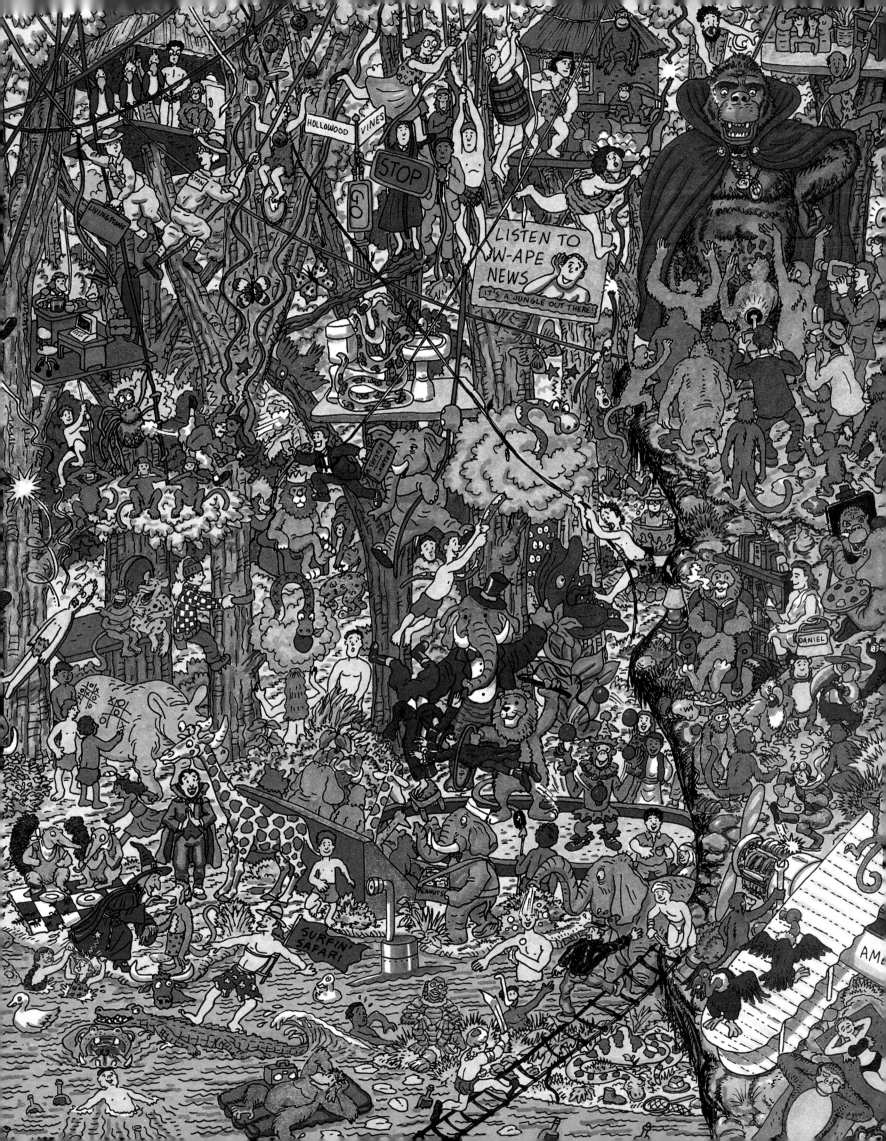

Pecos Bill was raised by coyotes out in the wild, wild west. When he grew up, he was the first cowboy to build a ranch and wrangle cattle. Once, Pecos Bill and his horse, Widow Maker, lassoed a cyclone!

First, find Pecos Bill. Then look for these other western things.

Pecos Bill

This cactus

An oil well

Sitting Bull

A "rattle" snake

This saddle

A coyote

This cowboy hat

Fr鸟m the time young Arthur pulled Excalibur from its stone, his life was filled with heroism, romance, treachery, and magic! King Arthur ruled with a fair hand. He was loved by many . . . and hated by a few.

Find Arthur and his trusted sword. Then look for Arthur's friends . . .

Arthur

Excalibur

Merlin

Sir Lancelot

Queen Guinevere

. . . and enemies!

Morgan le Fay

Mordred

Johnny Appleseed planted apple seeds across much of America before it was settled. He wanted to be sure that the settlers would never go hungry in their new homes. Sure enough, the settlers made up many apple recipes.

Can you find these delicious apple dishes? Look for Johnny Appleseed, too!

Johnny Appleseed

Apple pie

Applesauce

Apple cider

Apple muffins

Apple cake

Taffy apple

Fried apples

Apple dumplings

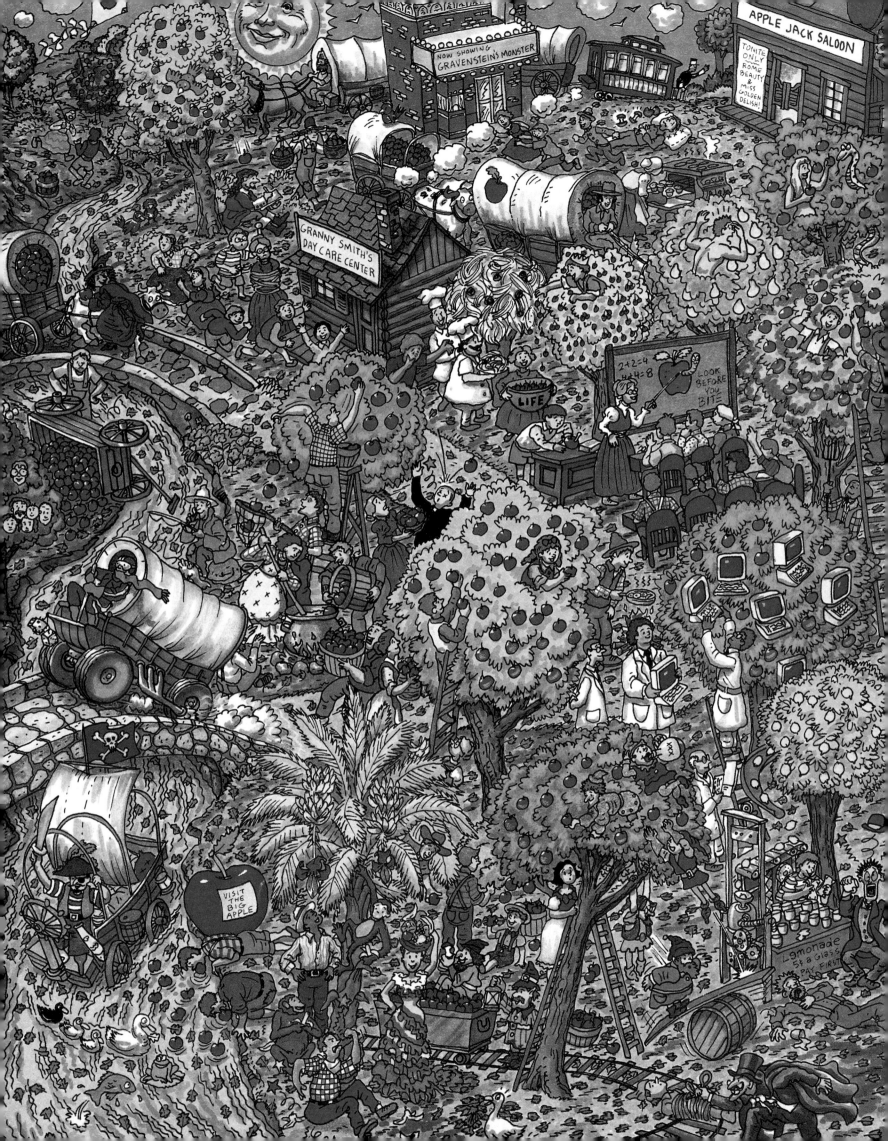

Hercules was the son of the mythical god Jupiter, but he lived on Earth among mortals. Hercules had superhuman strength. He performed so many wondrous feats that he was invited to live on Mount Olympus with his father.

Can you find Hercules? Can you find these other mythical gods?

Hercules

King Jupiter

Queen Juno

Apollo

Diana

Pan

Cupid

Mercury

Neptune

Scheherazade had made the sultan angry! But by telling him good bedtime stories, her life was spared. She told the sultan 1,001 stories in all. His favorite bedtime story was about Aladdin and his wonderful lamp.

First, find Aladdin. Then help the sultan find these things so he can get ready for bed!

Aladdin

Sultan

Royal pajamas

Night-light

Bedtime snack

Teddy bear

Storybook

Favorite pillow

Go back to the Perpetual Motion Ranch to find these cow and bull things.

- ☐ A cattle driver
- ☐ A bull"dozer"
- ☐ Cow punching
- ☐ A Spanish bullfighter
- ☐ A bullhorn
- ☐ A cow pie
- ☐ "Holy cow!"
- ☐ A "cow"ard
- ☐ A cow"lick"

Go back to Mount Olympus and help Hercules find these heavy things!

- ☐ A piano
- ☐ An elephant
- ☐ A safe
- ☐ A boulder
- ☐ A handbag
- ☐ Barbells
- ☐ A whale
- ☐ An anvil

Go back to King Arthur's castle. Can you find these royal things?

- ☐ A king cobra
- ☐ A "knight" club
- ☐ A kingpin
- ☐ A "knight" mare
- ☐ A princess phone
- ☐ A queen bee
- ☐ A royal flush
- ☐ A "knight" gown

Go back to Sherwood Forest to find these other "robbers."

- ☐ Ma "Barker"
- ☐ Bonnie and Clyde
- ☐ A horse thief
- ☐ The Knave of Hearts who stole some tarts
- ☐ A raccoon bandit
- ☐ Tom, Tom, the piper's son, who stole a pig . . .
- ☐ A cat burglar
- ☐ A ball player stealing home

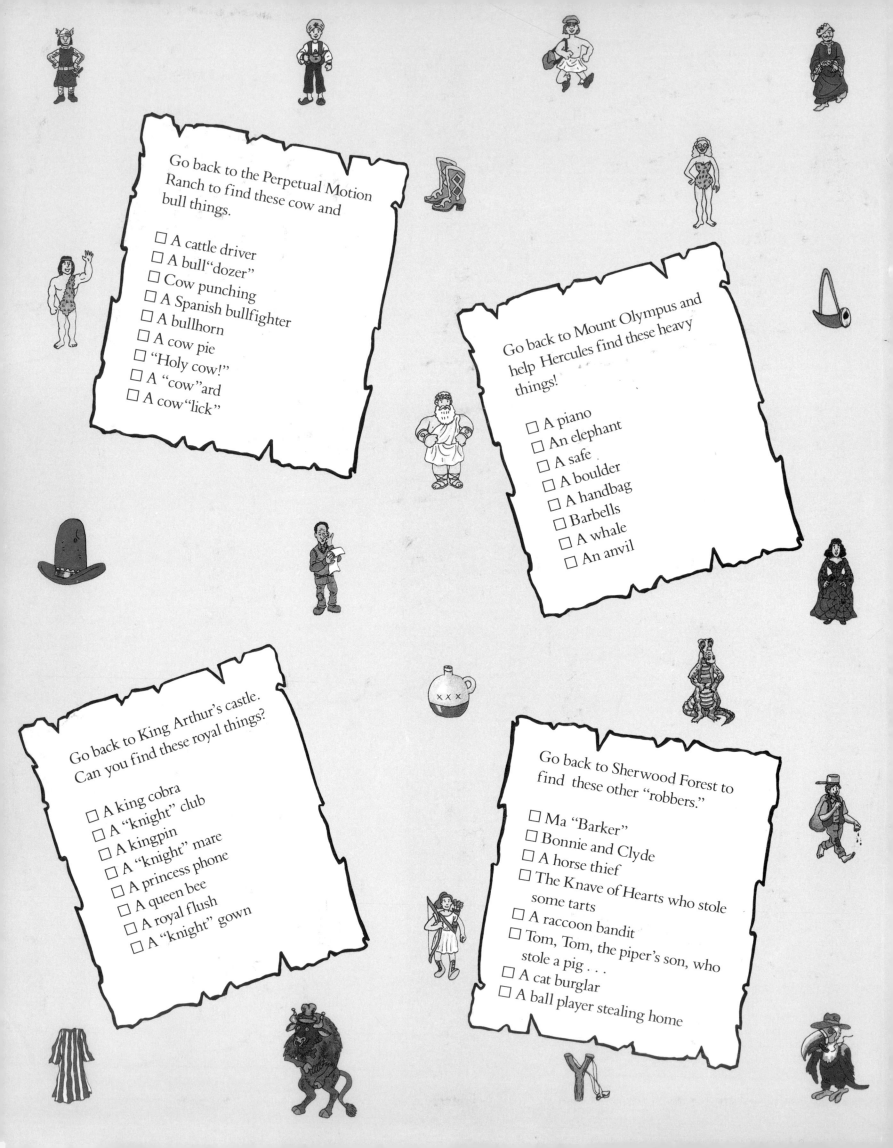

JORGE LUJÁN is an author, musician, and architect, who was born in Argentina and now lives in Mexico. He has published more than 40 books and has recorded 8 CDs. With some of the world's best illustrators he has created an outstanding body of work that has been translated into many languages. This includes *Trunk to Trunklet*, illustrated by Mandana Sadat, also published by Enchanted Lion. Jorge has received numerous awards and has been nominated for the Astrid Lindgren Memorial Award five times. More about him and his work can be found at www.jorgelujan.net. Look for Jorge Lujan on Facebook at Poesía y Música and on Soundcloud at Canción poética.

CHIARA CARRER was born in Venice in 1958. After high school, she traveled through Latin America for quite a while, engaged in both dance and theater. On her return to Italy, she moved to Rome, where she graduated with degrees in painting from the School of Fine Arts (Accademia di Belle Arti) and in engraving from the School of Ornamental Arts (Scuola di Arti Ornamentali). Since 1989, she has worked in high schools, setting up artistic laboratories. And since 1990, Chiara has devoted herself to children's book illustration. Her work has been honored with many prestigious awards and has been widely exhibited.

MARA LETHEM has translated novels by Jaume Cabré, David Trueba, Albert Sánchez Piñol, Javier Calvo, Patricio Pron, Marc Pastor, Toni Sala, and Alicia Kopf, among others. Her translations have appeared in *Granta*, *The Paris Review* and *McSweeney's*, and twice earned her English PEN Awards. She is a book reviewer for the *New York Times* and wrote the application that earned Barcelona designation as a UNESCO City of Literature. She has translated numerous books with Enchanted Lion, including the *Macanudo* series by Liniers.

There are many Pablos in the world, yet they all are one. Inside of each is a heart that beats with the same rhythm as the ocean's waves and the rotations of the planet.

Pablo was born in Chiapas, Mexico, and is now on his way
to the US border by train. His father was the first to cross,
followed by his mother. Both walking.

After two failed attempts, when border patrol sent him back,
Pablo sets out again. This time he wears his mother's
wedding ring around his neck.

Pablo looks at her, confused.
"Don't you want to?"
"Yes."
"But you don't."
"It's just that I'm missing things."
"What things?"
"A pencil... writing paper...
shoes... just things."

One day, a journalist appears and asks him, "How old are you?"
"I'm eight... nothing more."
"What are you doing in the garbage?"
"I'm looking for aluminum, cardboard...."
"To sell?"
"For food, that's what."
"You don't go to school?"

Pablo also scavenges in a favela in Río de Janeiro.
He spends his days picking through one of the city's
enormous garbage dumps.

Every day, Frejolito would give a cup of milk
to all the children of the poor families.
Everyone still remembers him.

"Imagine if he had become president," says Pablo.

Pablo also lives in Peru, the son of a teacher
who works in a small, rural school.
Pablo often talks about his godfather Frejolito,
who used to be the mayor of Lima.

And he writes. And he draws.

"Would you like somebody to get away
with doing that to you?" asks the poet.
Pablo looks at him, flustered.

A few moments later, Pablo picks up the sheet of paper
and rips it again and again and again.

One morning, a poet visits Pablo's school. "What do you want to be when you grow up?" the poet asks the children.

"I want to be a big guy in a uniform," Pablo replies.
"I see," says the poet.
"I didn't tell you why."
"Tell me, then."

Pablo draws in close to the poet and whispers, "Because I want to beat people up and get away with it."

"Oh," replies the poet. "Can you write that down and draw it?"
"No. You'll show it to my class and give it to the principal."
"I promise I won't show anyone."
"Okay, then, sure."

Pablo also lives in New York, the son of immigrants from Guyana.
He and his parents share a single room in the Bronx
with an aunt, an uncle, and four cousins, who recently arrived.
Each family has the room for twelve hours—
twelve hours in the room, twelve hours on the street.

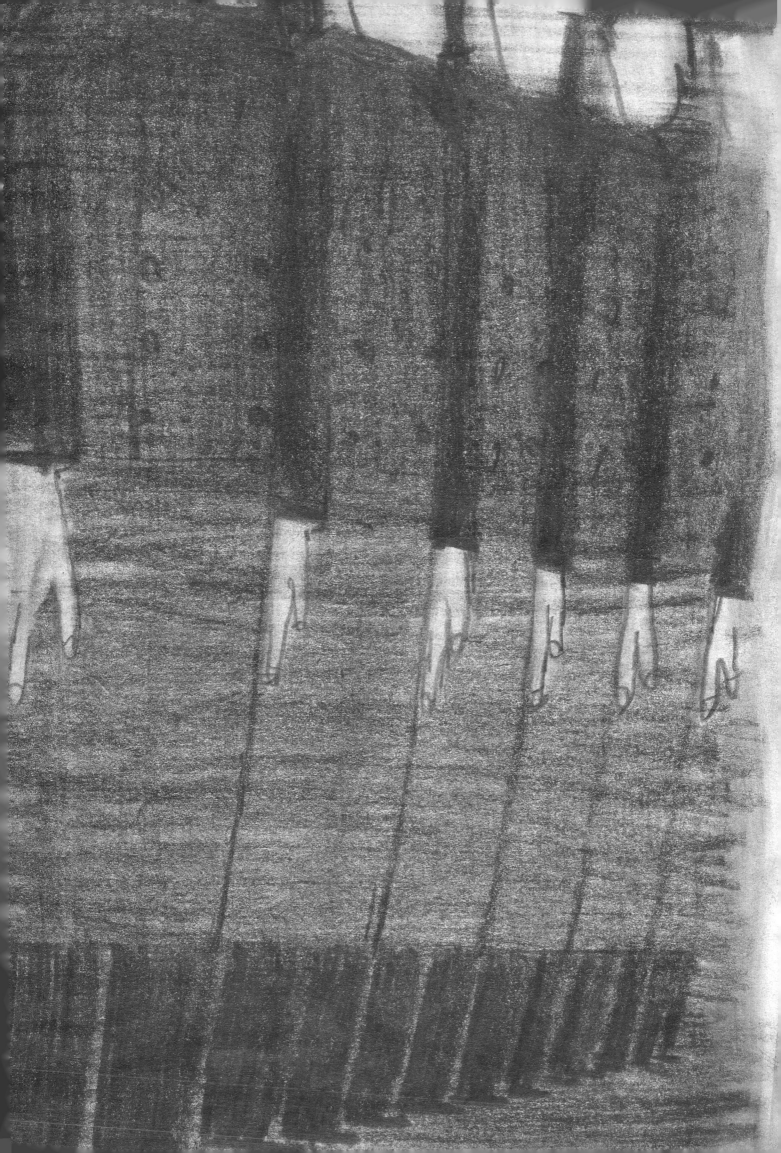

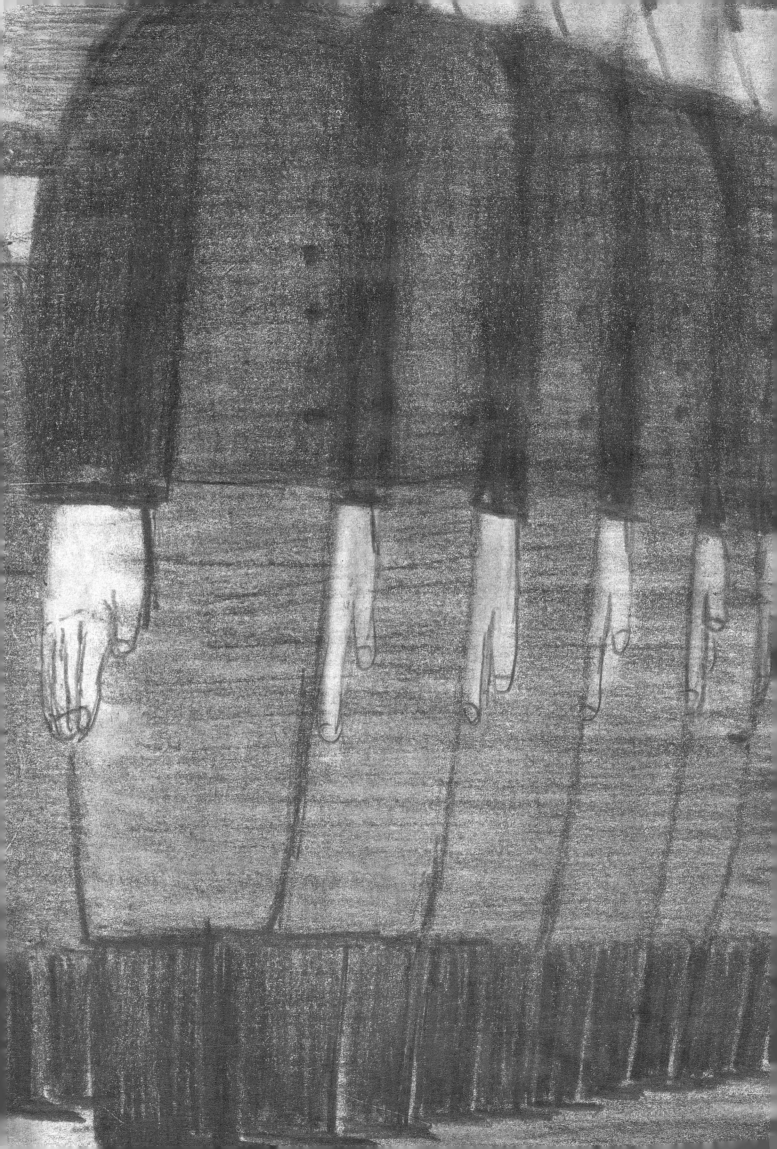

Pablo is an Argentine boy who lives in Mexico.
His parents took refuge there after escaping
the military dictatorship that ravaged their country.
Every day Pablo aches when he thinks about all
of his relatives and friends who have been taken away,
never to return.

On Thursdays he attends a poetry workshop
where he writes:

> Stiff and cold, the soldiers march,
> crushing the roofs
> with their enormous boots.

One day, a group of musicians cross the dry riverbed
and arrive in his village. They add their songs to the trills
of the jungle. Pablo and his mother are moved by their music.
Later, when the musicians drive off in their ramshackle truck,
Pablo and his mother run after them to share an orange.

"Don't forget us!" Pablo's mother calls out.
Pablo echoes her words, as the musicians vanish
into a cloud of dust.

There is also a Pablo living in Ecuador.
His home is in a part of the Amazon
jungle that is almost impossible to reach.
His mother picks fruit for a living.

When Pablo's father returns home, he quickly eats
whatever he can find and collapses into bed.

Pablo approaches, careful not to wake him.
When he puts his hand on his father's chest,
it feels like he's touching the center of the earth.

Pablo is eight years old and lives in Chile.
His father works in a copper mine,
where he spends his days drilling into the rock
half a mile underground.
It is cold down there, but he sweats nonstop.

SeVen PAblos

JORGe LujÁn   ChiArA CaRReR

Translated from Spanish
by MARa LetHEM

ENCHANTED LION BOOKS
NEW YORK

To Gianni Rodari.
To the children of the world.

—Chiara and Jorge

The poem by the Argentine child mentioned in the book
was writen by Haydèe Boetto, at 9 years old.

The art for this book was made with color and graphite pencil.

www.enchantedlion.com
First edition, published in 2018 by Enchanted Lion Books
67 West Street, 317A, Brooklyn, NY 11222
Text copyright © 2018 by Jorge Lujan
Illustration Copyright © 2018 by Chiara Carrer
Translation copyright © 2018 by Mara Faye Lethem
Art Direction: Claudia Bedrick

ISBN 978-1-59270-253-4

Printed in China by RR Donnelley Asia Printing Solutions Ltd.
First Printing

Feb 19

Going up

A hydraulic boom is like a telescope. It closes up when the crane needs to travel. When on site, fluid is pumped into the boom cylinder, forcing it to extend.

The operator sits way down here.

Stand still

The crane cannot balance on its wheels when the boom is extended. Strong metal outriggers are used to keep the crane stable.

7

Making tracks

Not every mobile crane moves on wheels. Some use **crawler tracks**, while others run on **rails**.

Heave ho... heave ho... heave ho...

It's snow problem

In the Antarctic, cranes with unusual crawler tracks are used to move equipment. The tracks stop the crane from sinking into the soft snow.

8

On the rails

Just as trains were invented before cars, the first mobile cranes ran on rails, not roads. Modern railroad cranes are used for laying and repairing tracks—and they no longer run on steam!

Tracks are also used on muddy or rough ground.

Under pressure

Crawler tracks spread a crane's weight over a large surface area. If it stood on wheels on soft ground, it would sink.

Towering above

Large **tower** cranes are fixed to the ground to stop them from falling over. The **tallest** freestanding crane stood **400 ft** (122 m) from hook to ground.

Swinging high

Saddle jib, or T-shaped, tower cranes move their loads by swinging their jibs around in a circle. This is called slewing.

Taller towers are tied to buildings for support.

Being at the top

Where space is tight, tower cranes with luffing jibs are used. These jibs move up and down as well as swing around.

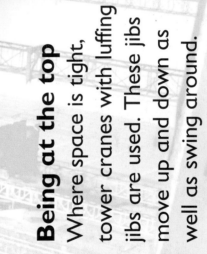

In control

A tower crane **operator** needs a good head for **heights**. Sitting high up in the crane's cab, the operator **controls** the movement of the jib.

Do look down

The crane operator needs to be able to see the load, which hangs below the trolley that runs along the jib. The cab turns with the jib to follow its swing.

Look out below!

Climbing frame
Tall towers have hoists that lift an operator up to the cab. But those who work on shorter cranes face a long climb up a ladder.

Lifting works

Mobile cranes and tower cranes are useful **outdoors**, but what happens when heavy goods need to be moved inside **factories**?

Off the wall

Jib cranes can be fixed to the wall or bolted to the floor like this one. The top arm, or jib, rotates to move the load.

14

The trolley rolls along on rails called girders.

Gird your strength

Some factories have girder cranes that run on rails near the roof. The crane's trolley scoots between the stockpiles and the trucks.

Unusual loads are carried on special kinds of hook attachments.

Freight lifters

The cranes at this **freight** terminal are used to load massive **containers** onto ships, ready for exporting overseas.

These stairs lead to the control cab.

Trolley time
The crane's load hangs down from a trolley, which sits on the boom below the cab.

The trolley carries its load toward the ship.

Container cranes are also used to unload ships.

A long reach

These cranes are ship-to-shore container cranes. The towers are lined up in a long row, and jut out over the edge of the docks to reach the ships.

Fast work

Before cranes, it could take weeks to load and unload freight from ships. Now it takes hours.

All at sea

Offshore crane vessels are the world's biggest cranes. These huge **floating** machines are important to the **oil** industry, as they help to build oil rigs.

This offshore crane vessel is based on the same design as an oil rig.

Load of goods

Oil-rig platforms are high above the sea's surface, so cranes are used to lift aboard supplies from boats. The boats get tossed around on the waves, so the cranes have to move fast to hook the load.

Carried aboard

It's not just supplies that arrive by crane: even the rig workers are lifted aboard from their boats. This is dangerous in rough seas.

Weighed down

Offshore crane vessels can lift oil rig parts that weigh thousands of tons (tonnes). The vessels use lots of anchors to stop them from moving around while they are working.

Log loads

You can't get wood without trees, but how do you get the trees from the **forests** to the **lumber mills?**

The crane's grapple picks up logs just like you would pick up a bunch of pencils.

These pine-tree logs could be used to make furniture.

Run of the mill

This gantry crane is similar to the ones seen at the docks. It has a big frame with a trolley that runs back and forth over the pile of logs below.

Pile 'em up

Once the trees have
been felled, they need to
be quickly piled onto trucks.
This loader crane is just like
an extra-strong, extended arm.

Bring your own

Some logging trucks have
their own built-in hydraulic
loader cranes. The crane
is controlled from its base,
just behind the truck's cab.

Helping hand

Lifting concrete **blocks** is all
in a day's work for many cranes.
But these machines can perform
much more **unusual** tasks.
Some are even out of this world!

Watch this space
An astronaut on a space
walk is tied to a type of
crane. It pushes him
around in space.

This arm connects to the
space shuttle's orbiter.

A green crane?
A crane helps with an environmental project by
lowering an old plane into the sea. The wreck
will create a reef, for fish and plants to live on.

The crane is
called a Space
Shuttle Remote
Manipulator System.

There's no land to walk on out here...

Moving house?
Not every house is built where it stands. This log cabin was made in a factory and transported by truck. It needs a crane to lower it into place.

People in the basket are tied in for safety.

Up for grabs

The **hook** on the end of a crane is very useful for lifting blocks, but how do you lift **mud** or even **people?**

Caged in
A personnel basket is used to carry people. The crane lifts them up to work in places they could not otherwise reach.

Spreader: this large clamp fits on top of a container. It is often used at the docks.

Orange-peel grab: the grab's fingers close tightly to stop the load from escaping.

Electromagnet: this powerful magnet will attract iron from a pile of scrap metal.

A dragline bucket is mainly used in mining.

It's a drag

This heavy scoop is called a dragline bucket. The crane pulls the bucket along the ground. Cranes that use these buckets are shorter and stronger than those that lift loads.

Days of old

Cranes are not a new idea.
Lifting machines were
used in ancient Egypt and Greece
more than **2,000 years** ago.

People power
Ancient cranes
were not powered
by electricity or
steam: they used
people. Slaves had
to turn the wheels,
which lifted the load.

Large cranes
today use
wire ropes
rather than
chains for
lifting.

The size of the
man gives an
idea of how big
the crane and
its load are.

Full steam ahead

This 100-year-old crane runs on rails and is powered by steam. Despite its age, it is still being used in India today.

Is anybody home?

Many steam cranes had large machinery houses—the case over a crane's workings. This one from 1900 looks like a house.

It's a fact

All cranes used to be made of wood. The first metal crane was made of cast iron in 1834.

The first steam crane was invented in 1839. Before then, a crane was powered by an animal on a treadmill or by a person turning a crank.

Picture gallery

Crawler tracks

These tracks stop the crane from slipping or sinking in the snow. Crawlers are mainly used on rough or muddy ground.

Loader crane

Hydraulic loader cranes are often mounted on trucks, but they can also be installed aboard ships.

Slewing grab

This crane, used in docks, has a double boom so it can lift heavier loads.

Mobile crane

This 18-wheel truck bears a crane that can extend 165 ft (50 m)—taller than eight giraffes.

Tower crane

The world's biggest tower crane, the K10000, can lift 117 tons (120 tonnes) —that's 25 elephants!

Dragline crane

Dragging a bucket over the ground is a different action from the usual lifting of loads.

Jib crane

Some factories have whole rooms full of these cranes—one at every workstation.

Spreader

This clamp is one of many crane attachments. Others include buckets for molten metal and suckers for glass.

Steam crane

Early steam cranes ran on rails. The first steam crane to drive freely, like a car, was invented in 1868.

Gantry crane

Gantries can have solid or lattice legs and beams. The first lattice was used in 1874, and is also used in other types of cranes.

Glossary

Boom a crane's long, extending arm.

Counterjib the arm of a tower crane that is opposite the jib. The counterweight and motors sit here.

Counterweight a metal or concrete block attached to a crane to balance the load and stop the crane from falling over.

Crane a machine that is used to lift items too heavy be moved by hand.

Crawler tracks a metal belt around a set of wheels on a machine, which helps it move over rough, soft, or slippery ground.

Freight goods that are transported to be sold.

Gantry a big frame that can be used to support a crane. Its bridge shape is designed to reach over obstacles.

Girder a strong, main support in a roof or other structure.

Hydraulics a system of operating machinery that uses fluid to push pistons to make the machine work.

Jib the arm of a crane that carries the load.

Lattice the crisscross pattern of metal bars that makes up a strong frame—but one that is lighter than solid metal.

Luffing the action of raising or lowering the angle of a boom or jib.

Outriggers the metal legs that support a mobile crane.

Slewing the action of moving a jib in a circle.

Trolley the part of a crane that runs along the jib. It has a hook attached to carry the load.

Index

Mobile crane

Acknowledgments

Dorling Kindersley would like to thank: Mechan Limited Sheffield for use of jib crane image, and Sarah Mills for picture library services.

Picture credits:

The publisher would like to thank the following for their kind permission to reproduce their photographs:

t = top, b = bottom, l = left, c = center, bgd = background

AKG Images 28cl; Alamy Images/Pictures Colour Library 4-5 bgd, /Leslie Garland 9b, /Maximilian Weinzierl 10-11, /Bo Jansson 25b, /Rolf Adlercreutz 26tl, /Pixoi Ltd 26bc, /David Jackson 30br; Alvey & Tower 14-15; Construction Photography/ Damian Gillie 1, /Anthony Weller 2-3, /Chris Henderson 6-7, 6t, /P.G. Bowater 11b; Corbis UK/Richard Cummins 7b, /Ecoscene/Graham Neden 8-9, 30tl, /Bob Krist 12-13, /Ralph White 16-17, 17t, /SABA/Tom Wagner 18-19, /Joel W. Rogers 18b, /Steve Chenn 21tr, /ChromoSohm Inc/Joseph Sohm 23tl, 30tr, /Amos Nachoum 24l, /Colin Garratt 29t, 31bl; Dorling Kindersley Media Library/Richard Leeney 5b, 30bc, 32; Getty Images/Robert Harding Picture Library/Mark Chivers 4l, 30bl, /Stone/James Wells 20l, /Christian Lagereek 31br, /Image Bank/Terie Rakke 22-23, /Michael Melford 22l, /Harald Sund 26br, /Photographer's Choice/Sandra Baker 26bl, 31tr; Robert Harding Picture Library/Premium Stock 19R; Mechan Limited Sheffield (www.mechan.co.uk), courtesy 14l, 31tc; QA Photos/ Jim Bryne 9t; Reuters/Kin Cheung 13t, Cheryl Hatch 16b; Science and Society Picture Library/National Railway Museum 28-29; Science Photo Library/Peter Chadwick 4bc, /NASA 24-25; Zefa Visual Media UK Ltd/E. Streichan 20-21, /Masterfile/Mike Dobel 26-27, 31tl.

All other images © Dorling Kindersley
For further information, see www.dkimages.com